Honey Eyes

Honey Eyes

A LONDON MYSTERY LOVE STORY

Kathryn Purnell

J R Garran

Title: Honey Eyes

Author: Kathryn Purnell (1911-2006)

First published in 2018 as an eBook
First Published in Print 2020

Copyright © J R Garran 2018

ISBN 978-0-6488606-1-7

A catalogue entry for this book is available from the National Library of Australia

www.trove.nla.gov.au

<h1 style="text-align:center">Honey Eyes</h1>

Colin Jepson's London adventure was the result of a chance decision. He could have selected his accommodation from a list supplied by an agent in the boarding house business. Instead, he responded to a suggestion from a fellow he met casually at Australia House in The Strand. An Australian himself, Jepson decided to take the chance advice of his fellow countryman.

Both men, having collected mail from Sydney, stood ten minutes to indulge the warm glow of reminiscence: George Street. Circular Quay, Woolloomooloo, Taronga Park Zoo, Palm Beach, Manly...

Then the stranger said to Colin: 'Last mail I'll be picking up. I'm going back tonight. B.O.A.C.'

To which Colin replied: 'Half your luck! I'll be here another six months.'

'Holiday?'

'No, not exactly, although the next four weeks will be in a way. In London, I mean. I'm on study leave from a graduate apprenticeship in Manchester.'

'Good on you. Where are you staying?'

'Nowhere yet. I've got a list of boarding houses – possibilities – in my pocket.'

'If they don't suit you,' the man said, 'try this. A friend of mine at home suggested the place but they couldn't take me at the time. Elm Tree Terrace.'

He handed Colin a card.

'I liked the look of the place and it's handy. An Aussie runs it, fellow by the name of Suddern.'

'Thanks. I'll write it down.'

'Oh, take the card. I won't be needing it again.'

No more than that, a mere toss of a coin, a look at the street map and a quick decision to try Elm Tree Terrace first.

The street was tree-lined, friendly-looking, and wide; the terraces gracious and full of dignity. The front of Elm Tree Terrace distinguished itself from its neighbours by a dark blue door with a round brass knob and nameplate polished to mirror splendour beside a healthy palm in a blue pot.

Colin rang the doorbell, was impressed by the resonance of its distinctive chime, and enquired of the maid if, by any chance, Mr Suddern might have a room available for an Australian from Sydney.

'Mr Suddern is out of town for the day, but if you would care to inspect it there is a room vacant. A gentleman left just yesterday for South Africa, sir. Miss Mary Mercy would look at your references sir, if you like the room. This way please, sir.'

The hall was thickly carpeted in a mute rose pattern and meticulously vacuumed. Mr Suddern did himself well.

'The lounge room, sir. Miss Mercy will see you here if you like the room.'

The same carpet flowed through the door of the lounge and met the folds of lined velvet curtains fading from rose to mushroom at the high window facing the street, opposite a massive marble mantelpiece under a mirror. Colin reflected on the height of the ceilings and sighed. Such grandeur was doubtless beyond his means. The maid continued down the hall to the junction where a second hall crossed.

'The dining room is that way, sir. Looks out on the garden. The kitchen's below. Inconvenient like, but Mr Suddern makes a point of food served hot. This way, sir.'

The quantity of 'sirs' forced Colin to attempt a closer look at his guide. Reluctantly his gaze fell from an architectural survey of architraves and chandeliers to observe the black and white figure of the maid, but he was thwarted as she preceded him around a right-angled elbow into still another hall.

'This way, sir. Here we are.'

Keys swung out from under the white apron, the door was opened, and the maid went inside and pulled back the curtains. The room and hall were flooded with light.

'Now, sir, if you would care to look at the room, I'll find Miss Mercy. Thank you.'

She was past him and into the hall again even as they stood in the doorway. She was older and heavier than her movements had previously indicated and he had to stand aside to let her past.

The dimensions of the room staggered Colin a little, but pleasantly. The ceiling seemed as high as the distance from the door to the window, though the room was no wider than the window itself. A second glance at the ceiling revealed the reason. There was no chandelier and only two corners sculptured in plaster. He was in an immense room he surmised, probably divided by window widths. The division to his right was built in with cupboards and bookshelves painted cream, which was also the colour of the window frames, the ceiling and the left wall. There was no bed but a divan with a head table that melted insignificantly against the solid wall. Like the single large armchair, the divan was featureless under a heavy loose cover, washed to nearly white. Save for a neutral-toned standard lamp shading a table and chair painted with the same brush, there was nothing else but the window framing the garden in oblong panes of glass. When night fell and the long beige curtains were shut, there would be no colour, Colin thought. For the drapes, like the seam-thin carpet, were faded to the toneless neutrality of dry grass in a summer paddock. He was drawn involuntarily to the window to bathe himself in the pale yellow sunlight that streamed into the room through the mottled branches of a giant elm. He might have been in the heart of outback Australia, the room was so silent and still. He had not considered before how much he had missed that lonely element. Whatever it cost, he decided he would take this room and recapture this strange sensation that concertinaed the distance between himself and home.

'Do you like the room?' a light voice asked.

He swung around in surprise. He had not heard anyone enter the room.

'I am Mary Mercy. You are?'

'Colin Jepson,' he answered mechanically. Then he narrowed his eyes slightly and smiled. 'Yes, I like the room.'

'You have references?'

'Yes, I have.'

Silence then, no more questions, no more words. He and Mary were poised like two hawks arrested in flight, appraising one another. Colin had never seen anyone like this young woman. She seemed to be tinted past the neutral shade of the room into gold, without the slightest trace of the pink and white of English beauty. Her skin was all one tone, two shades lighter than her hair. And she was long like himself and much too thin. Honey-coloured she was, with enormous liquid honey eyes. He drew in his breath in order to speak because her face was so serious and she did not allow her lips to answer his open smile, forcing him to reopen the conversation – he being the outsider whereas she belonged.

'What kind of references do you require?'

'Who sent you?'

'A man I met at Australia House recommended Mr Suddern.'

'What was his name?'

'I have no idea. I had other places to see and he suggested I come here if the others didn't suit me.'

'He stayed here then?'

'No, when he applied there was no vacancy.'

'It is a strange reference you offer, Mr Jepson.'

'My references, Miss Mercy, are in my pocket.'

Piqued he removed his wallet and opened it, slowly extracting, with deliberate preciseness, an envelope marked 'References'.

'I have here,' he said, 'letters from my bank manager, Sydney University, my medical adviser and my solicitor. Would you require any others?'

'Probably not. After I have read the letters, of course.'

He recoiled with a flash of unexpected anger at the tone of her voice.

After all, he was not trying to rent a room at Buckingham Palace. Her voice held an arrogance beyond the tone of insolence, yet even as he registered this, a softness flooded his mind, blotting out the insult he suspected, reducing his antagonism to pity. It was a totally unexpected somersault into compassion.

Baffled more by himself than by the young woman, he spoke without thought: 'Then read them, honey-eyes.'

'What was it you said? What did you say?'

Surprise in turn had driven from her tongue whatever pose she had assumed, exposing what he had unconsciously anticipated. What he heard was fear, which made him ashamed enough to have eaten the offending words.

'I'm sorry,' he said. 'You took me by surprise and I thought out loud. That is all. Your eyes are like honey and I'm only an average, susceptible male.'

Let her throw him out now if she wanted and be done with it. Her answer, however, did little towards sending him away.

'It doesn't matter,' she said, 'and it's better than being constantly connected with cats.'

'Cats?' he said, genuinely puzzled. 'Haven't cats got green eyes?'

'I wouldn't know about ordinary cats,' she said. 'I never had one and I don't want one. It's big cats, lions for instance, they seem to have eyes the colour of mine.'

'I only thought of honey,' he said, and felt ridiculously embarrassed, as if he were no more than seventeen. It didn't make it easier to see a tiny flash of colour rush up her cheeks to tint her cheekbones apricot.

The voice of the maid at the bend in the hall broke through the awkwardness, as startling as a motor revving on a silent street.

'Are you there, Miss Mercy? Shall I fix the room for the gentleman?'

No doubt whatever that he was staying. The first to sample supped, it seemed. He raised his eyes to the young woman's face again. Unaccountably she was trembling, her face turned towards the door, her body tense. He stepped up beside her, holding his references out in front of him towards her hand. She took them absently, straightened her shoulders, took a deep breath and called out: 'We're coming to the office now.'

Her voice had a forced note, as if she was annoyed at having to raise it above normal pitch in order to be heard. She followed her voice out of the room as if she considered herself attached to the last word, leaving Colin no option but to trail after her. She moved lithely before him down the hall, her feet noiseless on the carpet. He noticed her dress for the first time: cotton in a light mottled yellow, of a quality and texture unknown to him, sleeveless, almost roughly woven, and hanging loosely over her hips. Like her voice, it made him wonder.

'There's a lot to be done before they get back, Miss, and that will be soon enough. Mr Suddern said nine. Will you dine in? Seven o'clock in the dining room, sir.'

Colin started to speak. The young woman, pulled up by the solid presence of the maid blocking the hall, replied for him. 'There's plenty of time, Morris. Don't rush so or you'll be too tired to sleep.'

It was the mistress approach. The arrogance was there but it was gracious, kind. She has had servants all her life, Colin thought. Nevertheless, he decided to speak for himself. 'I'll dine in,' he said.

~~~
~~~

Dinner for Colin was a disappointment. Mary Mercy had read his references, accepted his cheque, and called a taxi for him for the purpose of collecting his luggage. Upon his return, Morris answered his ring and carried in his briefcases. The ports he carried himself, refusing Morris the privilege in spite of her expectant demand. No woman carried his luggage, not while he had two arms.

The curtains were drawn in the room, the bed professionally made under the divan cover. A decanter of water and two glasses stood on the table and towels hung below a mirror inside one of the wardrobe doors. These amenities were to be expected but it was a subtle change made in the room that held out to Colin a measure of promise, a hope that Mary Mercy might accept him in the dining room as a friend on equal, manageable terms – rather than the embarrassed girl who had fled before him down the hall or the aloof business woman who had ushered him out of the office to board his taxi. Mary Mercy in a dinner dress, green silk perhaps. She would look wonderful in rich, deep green. His gaze rested approvingly on the pot plant that made so much difference to the room. The table had been moved. It now stood out from the window, in the corner next to the bookshelves. There was room to place the chair between it and the curtains to look into the room at night. Or during daytime the chair could be placed on the other side of the table for a view of the garden. The pot plant, a magnificent specimen of an indoor rubber plant, broke the line of the curtains, the brick red pot and the saucer it stood in adding colour and life where none had been before.

He had grown restless before dinner and his anxiety made it seem a long time since yesterday, more than twenty-four hours since he had walked from Euston station at four o'clock in the afternoon, booked a room for the night at the nearest hotel, and then walked the streets until it was time for a meal. He had slept like a top in spite of the rumble of the trains. It crossed his mind to wonder how he would sleep this night, in this room, on the divan. The bookshelves went up and up towards the high ceiling. He noticed his meagre row of books looking minute and lost. For the first time in his life he felt houseproud. His mother, he reflected, would be highly amused.

Mary Mercy did not come into the dining room at all. But it was even worse than that. There was no place for her. There were three tables, each of which seated four people. He found himself with an elderly couple from Adelaide and a middle-aged school mistress from Scotland. Each of the other tables held married couples of various distinction. Except for himself it seemed that all the lodgers had rooms upstairs. They ate hurriedly in case they might miss an exceptionally good program on the television at eight. The school teacher assured him of a welcome in the lounge if he felt inclined to watch. She spoke with a genuine friendliness and a pleasant soft burr, but he was not soothed, though he could not bring himself to ask outright about Mary Mercy. Not even Morris appeared.

Dinner was served by an octogenarian in an ancient dress suit, assisted by a dumb-waiter that miraculously produced an excellent dinner for each guest in the order of their appearance. Colin judged that Morris was in charge below. On the grounds of fatigue he declined the invitation of Miss McKinnon and, as a preliminary move towards rising from the table, excused himself.

'You haven't had coffee, son,' remarked the man from Adelaide.

'Wait for it and take it to your room,' Miss McKinnon advised.

'You may have it here, or in the lounge, or in your room. There are no set rules, the Lord be thanked. I'd not be staying a minute if there were.'

'I gather the manager is away,' he said.

'It does not seem to matter one way or another,' he was informed by the wife of the man from Adelaide.

'It's Morris who runs the place. Neither Mr Suddern nor his partner appear to do more than give instructions to Morris.'

'I didn't know Mr Suddern had a partner. Miss Mercy signed me in. Is she Mr Suddern's partner?'

'Oh dear me no. Miss Mercy is Mr Suddern's niece. She's been staying here since the troubles in the Congo, you know, poor girl. Mr Suddern's business partner is Mr Huston. I understand Mr Huston is the silent partner, finance no doubt. Mr Suddern is the manager.'

'Huston's a queer fish,' remarked the man from Adelaide.

Miss McKinnon, like a diplomat, politely attempted to quash further conversation on a subject she considered outside the bounds of a reasonable interest in the affairs of an acquaintance.

'There are few enough places of this size and quality in the City of London where the guests avoid the daily scrutiny of the management of meals. I've had little to do with Mr Huston but I must say I have always found him a complete gentleman.'

'Just the same, I wouldn't trust him as far as I could throw him,' said the man from Adelaide. 'I suggest we have our coffee here, Mum, it's quicker.'

'Then I hope you will excuse me,' said Miss McKinnon. 'I'll have mine a little later in the TV room.'

When the waiter came Colin was relieved to ask that his coffee be served in his room.

'I'll be several minutes, sir. Will that be all right?'

'There's no hurry,' Colin said. 'No hurry at all.'

Mary Mercy did not bring the coffee as Colin hoped, nor did Morris. The elderly waiter brought it. Colin drank it while writing a letter home. At nine o'clock he walked out of his room to post it. The hall was brilliantly lit, almost dazzling after the dim glow of the movable standard lamp in his room. The voices from the television penetrated the air in canned waves of music and murmurs. He had not heard a tinkle of it in his room. The entrance hall was empty. The viewers sat in the lounge as one, without individuality, each face a receptive mask. Colin looked in at the door but Mary Mercy was not present. It surprised him slightly that Morris sat alongside the waiter on one of two straight chairs against the back wall. She spotted Colin immediately and flew to his side.

'There's a chair near the fireplace, sir,' she whispered.

'I'm not coming in,' he whispered back. 'I just want to know where to post a letter.'

'This side of the street. The corner to the right, sir.'

She preceded him to open the door.

'Thank you, Morris. Back you go.'

'Thank you, sir. There's supper at ten, sir, passed around in the lounge.'

'Thank you, Morris. Good night.'

It was not, of course, the first time a girl had taken over the mind of Colin Jepson. Dates with pretty girls were as natural to him as enjoying a good meal. He was studious. He had to be to get anywhere in his chosen profession, but he danced, played tennis, swam and sun-tanned himself whenever the time and opportunity presented themselves. His mother, he reflected wryly as he stepped out of Elm Tree Terrace, considered her son a wonderful catch and had advised him seriously before he left home to mind himself and be careful. His father had remarked that she need not worry, Colin had his head screwed on. So much for the loving faith of parents. With a dozen addresses in his pocket, not to mention the contacts he would make on the job here, he was on the first Friday night of his stay in London possessed by the eyes of a girl with whom he had exchanged a mere few words.

Significant words! All right! Honey-eyes, so where might this all lead?

At the postbox Colin disposed of his letter, turned on his heel, and with rapid strides set out towards the lights of a shopping centre where Expresso was written up in red letters. But he strode past the coffee bar, as alive with TV as Elm Tree Terrace, and instead of indulging in coffee walked for half an hour. It was a lovely cool night and he was sauntering and relaxed when he came back to the street of shops. In the High Street, a few yards down from the postbox, he bumped into Mary Mercy. She was not wearing green silk. She was in the same strange dress she had been wearing in the morning and she was in a hurry.

'Good evening, Miss Mercy.'

She stopped still in the middle of the street.

'Oh, it's you,' she said, and looked back towards the postbox and shivered.

'You should have a coat,' he said. 'You're cold.'

'I didn't have time for my coat. I'm running away.'

'You have no handbag either. You won't get far.'

'Far enough,' she said. 'I'll walk.'

'Are you going to friends?'

'Oh no.'

'You said you were running away.'

'Only for about an hour. He'll go to bed then.'

'Who, your uncle?'

'Oh no, my fiancé. Good night.'

She set off again in the direction of the shops. Colin caught up with her.

'Would it help if I offered you a cup of coffee at the Expresso there?'

'No, I couldn't do that. He might look there.'

'I see. Well would you like me to walk with you, then? I was only going back to bed anyway.'

'I suppose I could do that too.'

'What?'

'Go back to the house with you and go straight in my door as you go in yours. It wouldn't look odd, would it? My uncle hates anything that might look odd in front of the guests.'

'I presume the guests are in the TV room still.'

'Are they? Were they there when you came out?'

'Weren't they when you came out?'

'I don't know. I came out the dining room door and down the side path.'

'Well, can't we go back the same way?'

'It wouldn't look odd, would it?'

'Not to the guests it wouldn't if we happened to meet them; your fiancé might be different.'

'We won't meet him. He'll be in his room. He hates TV. He'll knock at my door but when I don't answer, he'll go back to his own room and after a while he'll go to bed, I suppose'.

'Furious, no doubt,' Colin said.

'Well then,' she said, 'he shouldn't send for me when I don't want to see him.'

'He sent for you?'

'Yes, he did. As soon as he got back he sent a note with Morris.'

'Is your uncle back?'

'Yes.'

'Then why didn't you go to him?'

'Because he thinks it's odd not to want to see my fiancé at night as well as during the daytime.'

'Well, isn't it?' Colin burst out.

She stopped and looked at Colin, so that he saw her eyes again. For a full minute. Then she sighed and her shoulders sagged.

'I see him for lunch and dinner. And afternoon tea as well. That's enough, isn't it?'

She began to walk again, slowly back towards the terrace.

It was like a dream and a childish fairy tale dream at that.

After a few steps Colin sought clarification.

'Are you engaged to marry your uncle's partner, Mr Huston?'

She replied in the same voice that had ordered Morris to stop fussing.

'It's all arranged,' she said. 'I agreed. Only I said that for the three months I only wanted to see Victor, that's Mr Huston, in the daytime.'

'And after the three months?'

'We'll be married. That's time enough to spend the evenings with him as well.'

Colin drew in his breath but they had reached the terrace. A small brick fence ran the length of the verandah and passed the narrow space between Elm Tree Terrace and the next house. Mary Mercy stepped over this fence and went down between the buildings. Colin stepped after her and followed closely. They arrived in the garden beyond the elm, crossed behind it and entered a door into the unlit dining room where she stopped, leaned back and whispered to him.

'I'm running away tomorrow afternoon as well. They've decided I need a drive, leaving at half past two. I'll be walking down High Street at two o'clock.'

Before he could answer, she had opened the door into the hall and he walked two steps behind her the full length of it, past the entrance hall to the elbow. The only sound was a subdued clatter of cups mingling with the voices of television. Abreast of Colin's door, Mary darted forward and put her hand on the next door handle. She turned her head to nod quickly before she went in. Colin stood in amazement until he heard her turn on a light and turn a key on the inside of the door. Her fiancé could have walked straight in through an open door to discover her absence but obviously this was not his custom. Apparently he preferred to send for her when it suited him. Colin decided that, like the man from Adelaide, he would not trust the fellow.

In Colin's room the lamp made the shadows dance. He decided to go to bed. Once in his pyjamas he opened the cupboard door that hid his hand basin and stood back, astonished to hear Mary Mercy cleaning her teeth. Resisting an impish desire to knock on the wall, he decided it was a simpler procedure to clean his own. By the time he finished there was not a sound on the other side of the wall.

Just the same, when he went to bed he left the cupboard door slightly ajar. But he could not sleep waiting, like a stupid, presumptuous Galahad, for the chance to rescue a maiden from some unknown terror of the night. Besides, after a sleepless silent hour, it struck him that his action could as well be interpreted as the rudeness of a lovelorn peeping Tom. Feeling like a fool, he got up, tiptoed across the carpet and silently closed the cupboard door.

~~~
~~~

The waiter wakened Colin, knocking on the door with morning tea at seven. At eight, Colin made short work of a hearty breakfast, after which he caught a bus into town, returning at noon just one half hour before lunch was served. His hands washed, his tie straight, he went into the lounge to wait. The man from Adelaide and his wife were sitting alone but before he could join them, he was approached by two gentlemen who appeared to be waiting to greet him.

'Mr Jepson? I'm Suddern, Fred Suddern. This is my partner, Mr Huston. I'm sorry I missed you last night – tried to contact you this morning. Welcome to Elm Tree Terrace.'

'Thank you very much, sir.'

'My niece tells me you come from Sydney, by way of Manchester. Studying here?'

'Post-grad appointment, sir, with a company.'

'Good. Well, glad to have another Aussie, aren't we, Huston?'

Victor Huston was a dark man, average height, average weight, even average years. He was a distinct contrast to Fred Suddern who signified decidedly his age and interests by a flaccid body, a prominent jaw-bone and a fleshy nose that proclaimed at a glance that his hobby was ale. His hair had once been as red as the present colour of his face and you could have picked him as stereotypical Australian anywhere in the world. He carried an invisible stock-whip for cracking purposes only, and an aura of living on the glory of the Australian Imperial Force. It struck Colin that Fred Suddern was about as out of place in Elm Tree Terrace as a man could be, while his partner was smooth enough to melt into any atmosphere as an owl into a tree.

'Care to crack a bottle with us before lunch?' Suddern asked.

'Not today, sir, if you don't mind. I have a date this afternoon.'

'Cripes, you haven't wasted any time, have you!'

Colin could feel Huston sizing him up. His eyes, small and deep-set under black brows, were keen as a lizard's. He spoke for the first time, his voice unexpectedly high-pitched and too English for a born Englishman. He ignored Suddern.

'In London for a holiday, Mr Jepson?'

'Partly, sir, but mostly work.'

Huston's eyes narrowed a little, perhaps at the use of the 'sir', which equated his age with Suddern's, but he grinned without humour. His teeth were very strong and white.

'Your lunch will soon be on.' He indicated the direction of the dining room with his hand. 'Come on, Fred, we wouldn't want to delay the boy for his date.'

Huston was the boss; there was no doubt of that.

~~~
~~~

At two o'clock, Colin Jepson was walking in the High Street. Mary Mercy approached him. She was wearing a straight beige dress and carrying a short green suede jacket. Her shoes and her handbag were of weathered lizard skin and the hair that rested on her shoulders was as smooth as a gold cap. You could have mistaken her neither for an English girl nor an Australian. Neither did she look American. Colin knew, as she walked towards him, that the side of her parentage not related to Suddern was European. There was something continental, not only about her clothes, but about the way she wore them – something German, perhaps, or Flemish. Yet her walk was as loose-limbed as a country road. She had certainly not grown up in a city.

There was a bus coming and the usual queue waiting to board.

Colin took Mary's arm and swung her towards the bus stop.

'Let's not be formal,' he said. 'Your name is Mary, mine is Colin. The top of a bus is as good a means as any to run away on Saturday afternoon.'

She held back, but he pushed her on, guided her upstairs into a seat and settled himself beside her.

'There you are,' he said. 'I've kidnapped you.'

'Don't say that,' she snapped. 'Don't ever say that again, I warn you. And I told you I hate animals, especially wild animals.'

'How old are you, Mary?' Colin asked bluntly.

'Too old to be dragged off to the zoo anyway.'

'The zoo!' Colin was dumbfounded. 'What zoo?'

'Whatever zoo this bus takes us to. I don't know. I might not seem very adult in your estimation, but I can read. This is a special bus marked "zoo". I suppose it's Regent's Park.'

'I'll ask the conductor,' he said and they sat in silence staring out the window so long that when the conductor came, Colin had changed his mind.

'Two to the terminus,' he said.

She tensed in the seat beside him but she didn't speak until Colin explained himself.

'I didn't know this bus went near a zoo,' he said, 'but seeing it does, I decided we might as well go there and let you have a look at the lions. Perhaps having looked at them, you will realise the colour of their eyes is not the same as your own.'

She did not turn her face from the window and when he glanced at her closely, he realised that she was crying without making a sound. He reached over and put his hand on hers.

'Mary,' he said contritely, 'come on, we'll get off.'

But she shook her head and the tears squeezed out of her eyes, and dripped onto her dress until finally she controlled them. Even then she did not turn to him, nor move her hand from under his. She just sat. Colin sat beside her and that was that, until the end of the journey. Then they got out of the bus and stood irresolute within sight of the entrance gate.

'We don't have to go in, Mary,' Colin said. 'We can just get a cup of tea somewhere. Don't you need a cup of tea? I do.'

'No, I don't,' she replied, drawing in her lip with sudden determination. 'You are quite right. I should go to the zoo. I need to see the animals again. Please buy the tickets. I haven't been to the zoo since I came to London,' she said. 'I was born in the Congo, in Kasai on my grandfather's estate. My father was born there too, and never knew or wanted to know any other home. He was a guide and a big-game hunter and like most of his breed, was too brave once too often. They didn't let me see my father, even at the funeral, nobody did, except the men who brought him in and my grandfather. I was twelve years old and neither my father nor my grandfather knew how much I hated the jungle, because even then I couldn't tell them, they loved it so much.'

'And your mother?'

'When my father was killed she had already been gone for years. She went away because she was sick – fear of the jungle made her sick with terror day and night. She never let me see her fear. I only knew because my grandfather told me later.'

'She was Mr Suddern's sister?'

'Yes, she came back here to live at Elm Tree Terrace, but when my father finally refused to join her, she went back to Australia and died there three years later. My uncle stayed on as manager. He thought she would come back. You see Elm Tree Terrace is my grandfather's London House for leave and such.'

'Funny,' Colin said, 'somehow I didn't think you were English.'

'Oh, I'm not. Grandfather is Belgian. He went out to the Congo in 1910 – I suppose you could say he was one of the original idealists who opened up King Leopold's kingdom. My Grandmother was English. He bought the house for her. He hates it here. He longs for the jungle – he is dying for the need of it. I'd take him back if I could.'

'Hating it as you do?'

'Even for me it would be better than the terrace.' She sighed. 'But he is too ill to go back, and even if he could, it's not allowed and there is no place to live. All the buildings are burned down. Only Grandfather and I came out with our hands. That's what broke his heart. That's why he is dying. The doctor says, six weeks, two months – three months at the very longest.'

'Three months,' Colin repeated, shocked beyond words remembering Huston, who was waiting for this chance to get Mary. He put his hand under her elbow as they walked.

'He is in the hospital then, your grandfather?'

'Oh no, at least not that. He is at Elm Tree Terrace in the room next to mine. He has had a stroke and cannot speak. He just lies there all day, waiting to die. He doesn't want to go to hospital so we look after him there, my uncle, me and Morris, and Victor of course.'

For something to say to break his own appalled silence, Colin asked: 'Who was in my room before yesterday?'

'A business associate of Victor. He flew back to Katanga. He said he was going to Capetown to buy diamonds, but really he's going to Njolo to cross the border.'

'Do you think, Mary, that if your uncle or Victor Huston had been at home, they would have rented his room to me?'

She stopped to consider this. Then she said simply 'Why not?'

'Because of your grandfather. Everybody else is upstairs. The last tenant was a personal friend of Huston's.'

She was silent again, thinking before she replied. 'Well,' she said then, 'you're my friend.'

'They don't mind, your uncle and Mr Huston?'

'They haven't said so. Why should they?'

'Mary, they are going to mind, after last night and this afternoon.'

'I don't think so. You see, they are used to me running away because of Grandfather and they know nothing can make any difference.'

'To what?'

'To me marrying Victor, when Grandfather dies.'

'Does your grandfather know?'

'Yes, you see, sometimes he is a little better and I tell him things and I can tell from his eyes that he understands.'

'Mary, why are you marrying Huston?'

'Because I have to, for Grandfather's sake.'

'He wants you to?'

'He thinks I want to and he is pleased for me to be looked after.'

'And do you want to?'

'Of course not.'

It was like talking to a woman in her sleep and Colin, suddenly infuriated, removed his hand from her elbow and strode ahead of her. A group of children laughing with excitement ran by, taking him with them until he forcibly extricated himself and looked back to see if Mary had been run down by their boisterousness. His eyes located her sitting on a bench staring into an enclosure of flamingos that he was sure she did not see. He walked back and flung himself on to the seat beside her.

'You are angry,' she said. 'I'm sorry.'

'I'm sorry myself,' he said. 'I can't understand you.'

'I don't understand either. I've talked so much to you. I only talked to myself before, even at home. I never knew anybody like you.'

'But you must have friends, girlfriends, older people?'

'No, there was nobody my age at home, except the natives, of course. There was only Grandfather and myself.'

'But at school?'

'I didn't go away to school. I went to the Convent for a time while

Grandmother was alive. She was going to send me abroad to school when I was ten or eleven. But Grandfather didn't want me to go away. He taught me himself with Monsieur Vernier and Father Paul. I wrote my exams at the Convent.'

'It's a wonder,' Colin exploded, 'that you aren't a nun already, instead of the future wife of a man twice your age.'

Then he was aghast at himself, remorseful and chagrined to have attacked her religion, which was probably the only solace she had. But she hadn't even that.

'Are you a good Catholic, Colin?'

'No,' he said.

'Grandfather is a free-thinker,' she said, 'a humanist, but Grandmother was an Anglican. I don't think I'm anything at all. Religion missed me.'

'Missed you?'

'Yes, it's sad in a way, at least I used to think so. It doesn't matter very much now. Sister Monica, the Mother Superior talked to me about it, and Father Paul. They were such good people considering I wasn't even baptised. They did everything they could for me, but Grandfather would not have me taught religion. That's why he took me away from the Convent when Grandmother died. But Grandfather supported the Convent, they could always come to him for money right until the end.'

'It's unbelievable, absolutely unbelievable. You yourself are unbelievable Mary Mercy. If I told any single person what I know about you, they simply wouldn't believe me.'

'Oh well,' she said, 'I'm not surprised. Uncle Fred has already told me I'm odd.'

'Odd,' he breathed and his heart suddenly filled his throat so that he choked. 'Not odd; you're wonderful, Mary Mercy.'

She laughed a funny strained little gurgle, like a first experimental trill from the throat of a thrush in spring.

'Mercier,' she said. 'How could I be called Mary Mercy? That is a saint's name.'

He began to laugh with her then, an intoxicating gladness surging up from his heart.

'I thought Morris called you Miss Mercy.'

'She does, but she can't help it. She can't speak French.'

Suddenly, hopelessly, infectiously they laughed aloud. It was like a dam bursting, a great flow of irresistible pressure carrying them off together. People walking past stared only to smile and pass on, thinking them lovers lost in some ridiculous personal phase of delicious uncontrollable mirth.

'I must tell you, I know I should,' Mary spluttered between spasms, 'that I know my eyes really are the colour of a lion's eyes, except that mine don't send telegrams when I'm angry.'

'What?' Colin gasped.

She grew suddenly stiffly serious.

'Didn't you know,' she said, 'when a lion is angry, he gives warning. His eyes go almost black. A leopard's eyes don't change, which makes him more dangerous. You see Colin, I am cheating. I have been as close to a lion as I am to that flamingo. I have stood beside my grandfather and watched a lion shot through the eyes. I was always afraid – always, Colin – even though the lion was not angry, made no sign, simply stood perfectly still waiting to be murdered.'

'Murdered? Shot, you mean.'

'No, my grandfather never let a lion escape, not after Father. That's what frightened me, Colin. That's why I can't look at a lion. There were nights when, in my dreams, prides of lions surrounded our house, snarling for revenge.'

'Is that why you didn't want to come to the zoo?'

'In a way but not really. I don't hate lions, and zoos are just a kind of educational picture book to me. You wouldn't know Lake Kivu would you? No you would not.'

'I've heard of it.' He resented feeling like a schoolboy in a geography class. 'But I can't say I'm sure where it is.'

'I went to Lake Kivu with my father year after year when I was a child.

In the Rift Valley the herds run in thousands and on Lake Kivu the birds rise in millions. They darken the sky. It's hard to explain at a zoo.'

'The same thing in millions is still only the same thing,' he said sullenly. He felt himself seething with annoyance for being obliged to insist that the roar of a lion behind bars was the same as a predator on the kill; that a stationary flamingo balanced on one leg was a sight that rivalled the sunset. But he was caught in some grotesque contradiction within himself. He had fallen in love with this girl and the lions he had never seen surrounded him too. She didn't want to argue or even commit herself further, but he could not let her be.

'The trouble is you've seen too much of nature in the raw.'

She turned her honey eyes up to his own with patient resignation and he knew that some hidden truth lay in the opposite; that for his own part, he had seen too little to balance her fears. She spoke softly to him as if she sensed his frustration.

'I didn't go again after my father died. He adored Kivu. It's the kind of place that puts a spell on people.'

'That seems to be an African characteristic.'

'Not everywhere – not in Kasai where I lived.'

'Where? Oh let it go – wherever it is put a spell on your grandfather didn't it. He could have left with all the other Belgians couldn't he?'

'Yes, he could have. But he wouldn't. He wanted to die there for all he believed in. It was different for Grandfather.'

'I can't say about that. But I can say it all sounds to me like the wrong place to bring up a girl. None of it sounds like women's terrain.'

'Where there are men, there are always women, Colin.'

He thought suddenly of the dry, waterless waste of outback in New South Wales where his Uncle Joe ran sheep and his Aunt Myrt grew hard-faced and shy with loneliness, miles from the nearest neighbour. He grinned.

'Ever hear of a place called Milparinka?'

'No,' she said.

'Then we're quits. It's in Australia, in New South Wales.'

'Is it a place like Lake Kivu?'

'The very opposite. There's no water at all, only bore water.'

'Bore water?'

'Underground. You sink a bore, like a well.'

'Is it desert?'

'Oh no, it's sheep country.'

'Bushman country, like the Kalahari?'

He would not allow himself a further geographical involvement.

'My aunt and uncle have a sheep station out from there. It's a God-forsaken place. I hated it – it seemed like the end of the world.'

'Sometimes you feel just as God-forsaken when everything is lush with beauty. It is too much for every day.'

When she looked at him, the pale topaz of her eyes seemed shadowed with unshed tears.

'When what I dreamed happened, Colin; when we were surrounded – it was not by lions. They don't leave their own territory to kill. Only men do that. It was lucky for us that Grandfather was more respected for the lions he had killed than for the men he had not. Can you understand that?'

'Mary, Mary dear, you don't have to tell me.'

'I know. But I want to tell you. I never wanted to tell anybody before.'

'Go ahead then, let it out,' he said, 'except don't tell me again that you have lions' eyes.'

'My eyes don't matter. There are good lions and bad lions; good men and bad men. You don't need to worry about either of them – they stand out and you can tell. You are good, Colin – my grandfather is good. It is the others, the mixtures of good and bad – the ones who might jump either way that are so frightening. Grandfather always said the natives were more good than bad, that they only needed help and leadership. He used to hold Kuba wood carvings in his hands and explain how clever these people were, building movable huts in their ancient tradition. He respected them and they respected him. But he knew just how near the surface of tribal life lay the rituals of cannibalism and the chaos of inter-tribal feuds. He feared independence because he knew the country was not ready for it. When the fighting broke out in Kasai between the Baluba and the Lulua, he told me everybody would suffer and that he had to take his chance and stay to help those he loved from making beasts of themselves. And he was right Colin. Our people stood by him. It was a wild barbaric riot of marauding strangers that burned and looted our home, egged on by the broadcasts of half-educated power-seekers who promised every kind of loot including white women. Our servants saved us. They gave my grandfather a drink that put him to sleep and carried us both in the night to their village to hide us. And all the way they chanted – I will always hear them: "Save the old lion-killer and the girl of his heart. His gun protected us from the lion. The old lion-killer must not die." One of our boys even packed two suitcases, pretending it was loot, which were found beside us when we were dumped where Europeans would find us. They carried us for two days and nights to their village to hide us and more days and nights to get us away. There were strange things in the suitcases, Colin; touching, unexpected things, like a moth-eaten teddy-bear I had not handled since I was a child, which perhaps they thought was my totem, and my grandfather's eightday clock. But there were none of their own carvings or woven textile pieces that my grandfather had collected with such loving care. Grandfather came to, on the aeroplane. He has not spoken since. My uncle met us at the airport and brought us to Elm Tree Terrace. Doctor Finter came at once to see him and told Victor, who was living here at the time, that Grandfather had suffered a stroke and would not speak again.'

Quite suddenly a lion roared and Colin jumped as if the great cat had sprung upon him. But Mary Mercier sat staring at the pink flamingo she did not see. The roar of a lion meant to her a lesser evil.

Very gently Colin Jepson placed his hand under Mary Mercier's arm and raised her to her feet. Then, with his arm around her waist, he led her out the gate. Three taxis and two buses stood at the kerb. Colin whistled. In the back seat of the cab, isolated from public gaze, he kissed her.

'I know it sounds impossible so soon but I love you, Mary,' he said. 'I want to take you home with me to a country as warm as your own and perhaps, in its way, just as beautiful. I am sure there are no wild beasts there and I will try to protect you from human beasts for the rest of our life.'

'You cannot protect me,' she whispered, 'but thank you for loving me. It is enough.'

'It is not enough, my darling, but I suppose it will have to do for now.' Colin sat up very straight. 'Tell me why you have promised to marry Victor Huston.'

'My uncle owes him money, owes him all of Elm Tree Terrace – which is all my grandfather has left to give to me. The only thing that remains for Grandfather when he dies is to know that I own Elm Tree Terrace.'

'The dirty blackmailers!'

'I didn't care, Colin. As long as Grandfather can die in peace, thinking I am happy and provided for.'

'It's a monstrous price to pay. Do you think your grandfather would have you sacrifice your whole life for such a thing? Would he have you be a hostage?'

'He must not know.'

'If we tell him, Mary, that we love each other, that I will look after you?'

'He would not understand that I could live without means, without servants. Victor is rich, which makes Grandfather content. He has promised to redeem with his wealth all we lost in Africa. Victor has been kind, very kind to Grandfather. He is very strong. He lifts Grandfather in his arms and makes him comfortable. Grandfather trusts him.'

'Oh, my poor darling,' Colin said. 'Any nurse could lift him. I could lift him.'

'He must not be sent to hospital. I have asked him again and again in every way I can but always he shakes his head. He wants only two things: to know I am well provided for and to die at Elm Tree Terrace. How can I wish him to live like he is? He was so vital, so strong, so wise.'

Colin was young and his passions blinded his senses.

'And for this,' he said with the bitter cruelty of love, 'you will sacrifice yourself – and me. O.K. then, if that's how you want it.'

A few minutes later he stopped the taxi in the High Street at the letterbox, let Mary return to Elm Tree Terrace alone as she had departed, while he walked into the Espresso Bar and filled in time with several tasteless cups of black coffee. His anxiety was such that he was restless to return and yet when he let himself in to the muted veldt colour of his room, he hated the tawny beige of its neutrality. His eye fell on the rubber plant in the red pot, which seemed to him like a bleeding sore that would not heal. He opened the long window and pushed the plant outside onto the brown earth under the elm. A young lion himself, he paced the distance between the drawn curtains and the door without lighting the lamp against the dusk. Once, as he heeled round, he jerked open the cupboard door and heard what he'd hoped to hear: a rhythmic muffled sobbing like wind trapped in a hollow space.

'I can't. I can't love her like this and abandon her,' he told himself, but he was without the power of his reasoning mind and he knew his emotions were beating his brain to pulp.

Then, quite suddenly, he could no longer tolerate himself in the room, even in full darkness. He opened the door and went out into the full neon glare of the hall and the voices of the television. Dinner was over but the tinkle of cups and the aroma of coffee confirmed the early hours of the evening. He was amazed that it was still so early. Coffee!

There was only one person in the reading lounge. The magnet of TV had drawn all the others like pins into its presence. Only one had escaped to sit now, facing the hall door in apparent contentment behind an enormous newspaper. It was the man from Adelaide.

He looked straight at Colin, over the top of his glasses as he put down his paper.

'Hello, son,' he said. 'You sick?'

'No,' Colin said. 'If the coffee is off, I'll get myself a cup down the street.'

'Mind my company? I want cigarettes.'

'I'd be grateful, sir,' Colin said and was surprised at himself, recognising that out of the whole house, and out of the whole of London, the only one he could talk to – the only one who mistrusted Victor Huston –

was this man, old enough to be his father, a fellow countryman this small, ordinary, keen-eyed businessman from Adelaide

On the street, Colin offered him a cigarette.

'I'm a pipe man,' was the answer received. 'But you said—' Colin began.

'I know a bit about boys of your age. You're in trouble. I saw you come in before dinner. You didn't eat. It's your business, but if you want a pair of ears then talk; if you don't, say so.'

'I'd like to talk,' Colin said. 'God, I'd like to talk but I don't know where to begin.'

'Start with the girl. It's the little Belgian girl from the Congo, isn't it?'

'But how—' Colin began again.

'I was coming down the street to the post,' said the man from Adelaide. 'I saw the taxi stop. Miss Mercier nearly knocked me down. I doubt if she knows she bumped me even yet. I'm interested in that little girl, so is Mum. There's something fishy going on in Elm Tree Terrace and I don't know as I'm too anxious to see a boy from home mixed up in it.'

'She's mixed up in it,' Colin said, 'and she can't escape – she's trapped.'

'And you are Sir Galahad? You know Mum said to me "if that little girl sees that young man..."'

'It's not funny, sir, I've fallen in love with her.'

'And she?'

'Is going through with marrying Huston.'

'That snake in the grass! Begin at the beginning, son. We'll walk. Be as brief as you can because when we come to a likely looking place, we'll get you a meal. Then walking back, we'll try and figure out a solution. It's a method of mine. Walk and state the problem. Stop and eat in silence, walk again and plan your next move.'

In spite of his anxiety, Colin cast a quick appraising look at the little man from Adelaide. The tension in him eased. Colin began to talk.

~~~
~~~

Notwithstanding the reassuring optimism of the man from Adelaide, Colin spent a restless night. Sleep, when it eventually came, was troubled with a succession of lions, superimposed alternatively upon the dream-forms of Mary Mercier and Victor Huston. The morning burdened Colin with a headache and a restlessness he had never known before. It seemed, at breakfast time, an impossibility to follow the plan: physical in-activity agreed upon the night before between himself and the man from Adelaide. To sit around in the lounge and the TV room, to inquire of Morris as to the whereabouts of Mary, to act lovelorn and distracted, seemed to Colin by the light of the day, a nauseating procedure. Mr A W Conway, the man from Adelaide, however, seemed if anything normal to the point of banality. At breakfast even his voice was genial. As he stood up from the table he pulled out his wife's chair and loudly invited Colin to come up and see his rooms on the second floor.

'Almost a suite we have, you know,' he said. 'Our own little sitting room, not so big but it has a couch, two armchairs and a table. As usual, Mum has a display of family photos to bore visitors with. Like to see them? Come at eleven for a drink – give me a chance to polish off my business letters first.'

'Thanks very much,' Colin said stiffly. 'I'd like to.'

'We never thought Mr Conway could be so gregarious,' Miss McKinnon remarked to Colin, leaving the dining room. 'Generally he is a most abrupt man, almost to the point of rudeness. Something must have happened to cheer him up. Business prospects, I hope.'

'I wish something would happen to cheer me up,' Colin replied. 'I could do with it. By the way, Miss McKinnon, you haven't seen Miss Mercier this morning, have you?'

Miss McKinnon, in spite of her usual demeanour of detached and friendly interest, raised her eyebrows.

'No, Mr Jepson, I have not. You could try the office.'

'Oh it doesn't matter,' Colin said. 'I heard her old grandfather had a bad turn, that's all.'

'Indeed, I am sorry. Poor old gentleman. Has the doctor been again since yesterday, then?'

'I didn't know he came yesterday,' Colin said.

'He came as usual, but although I had the pleasure of a few words with him before dinner in Mr Huston's company, I had no idea there was a deterioration in Monsieur Mercier's condition. How very distressing. I did not even inquire about the health of the old gentleman.'

'Well, you couldn't know,' Colin prompted, smiling straight at Miss McKinnon with the innocent eyes of a schoolboy.

'Oh but, Mr Jepson, I should have inquired because I did see little Miss Mercier running down the passage past the lounge-room door, and I should have guessed.'

'But how could you, if Mr Huston didn't say anything?' He paused. 'But I expect you mean you should have asked the doctor when Mr Huston left.'

'Mr Jepson, I didn't say Mr Huston left.'

'What, not even when his fiancée ran down the hall?'

Miss McKinnon regarded Colin with undisguised amazement, her eyebrows this time unmistakably arched.

'I don't think I understand you, Mr Jepson,' she said.

'Oh, didn't you know Miss Mercier was engaged to Mr Huston? I thought everybody knew.'

'I am sure I don't know who could have made it their business to give you such information, Mr Jepson. My opinion would be that if such an attachment exists, neither Mr Huston nor Miss Mercier would feel an announcement at the present time would be fitting.'

'Mary Mercier told me herself,' Colin said, 'so I don't think they mind. I must say, it seems strange to me – Huston is old enough to be her father. He's your age, not hers.'

'Mr Jepson!'

'She's not as old as I am and she isn't in love with him either,' Colin exploded into her shocked face. Excuse me, I must find Morris. See you at lunch.'

He left Miss McKinnon standing aghast in the hall and hurried to the office, and from the office to the television lounge. He found both rooms deserted, which he had expected. Back in his room, he collected a book and then, with a degree of nonchalance he did not feel, settled himself in the coffee lounge in the chair which last night had been occupied by Mr Conway of Adelaide. It offered an excellent view of the front hall and he remained there until ten minutes to eleven when Morris walked by with her hat on.

'Morris!'

She came back and stood in the door. 'Yes, sir?'

'Morris, I heard Miss Mercier's grandfather had a bad turn in the night. Would you give Miss Mercier my regards and tell her I hope he is better?'

There was a long pause and then Morris said, 'Now, sir?'

'Yes please, if you don't mind, unless the doctor is with him of course.'

'I don't know what's got into this house this morning, sir,' Morris snapped. 'Miss McKinnon inquired for the old gentleman's health and then Mrs Conway and now you.'

'Then I'm sure you won't mind giving Miss Mercier my message.'

'She's not *in*, sir.'

'Not in! Good heavens, she hasn't gone for the doctor again, has she?'

'Certainly not, sir. The doctor will come at his usual hour. The old gentleman is quite as well as usual, sir.'

'You gave me quite a start,' Colin said. 'Don't worry, Morris. As long as Miss Mercier has only run away again, her grandfather must be all right.'

'Sir?'

'That's all, Morris. Just give Miss Mercier my message when you see her. Only privately please, Morris, not when her uncle or Mr Huston is present.'

An incredulous expression flitted across the face of the maid. Then she bent her head to one side, as if she found herself unexpectedly deaf.

'Excuse me, sir,' she said. 'The bell. I think I heard a bell.'

She left him and went back the way she came, her hat bouncing on her head.

At eleven, Colin left the lounge and went up to the suite of the Conways of Adelaide.

~~~
~~~

During lunch, two couples made inquiries of Mrs Conway concerning the health of Monsieur Mercier. Neither Mrs Conway nor Miss McKinnon appeared to have any further information to offer, or if they had, they considered it polite to withhold it. Conway, however, addressed his wife in his usual abrupt and cynical manner, only his voice was louder than usual.

'If you ask me, Mum,' he said, 'they ought to see our specialist. I'm not impressed by that medico who comes to visit. Shifty-looking.'

Miss McKinnon took it upon herself to reprimand him, politely of course.

'Why, Mr Conway, Dr Finter is an old personal friend of Mr Huston's.'

'All the more reason'. was the response.

~~~
~~~

By six-thirty, Colin was fatigued, depressed, deflated and thoroughly bored with sitting morosely in the Elm Tree Terrace lounge. The hours, however, had been well spent. Everybody in the house knew he had fallen in love with Mary Mercier and that she was engaged to marry Victor Huston – a man old enough to be her father – for reasons unknown as, according to rumour, she was not in love with him and was eating her heart out for Colin. This situation presented intrigue which, combined with the bad turn the old gentleman had apparently suffered in the night, held better dramatic possibilities for the guests than television. To the disgust of Suddern and Morris, everybody was unexpectedly present in the lounge for afternoon tea and showed little sign of departing before dinner. One by one they tried to cheer Colin up, only to be rebuffed. Miss McKinnon, Morris remarked to Suddern, was already dressed in her black silk with three rows of pearls. Colin had made no move to occupy any but the one lounge-room chair that faced the door, and when Fred Suddern or Morris looked in at frequent intervals, all eyes looked up expectantly hoping to see Mary Mercier for the poor boy's sake – as well as the gratification of their own curiosity.

Mary was said to be indisposed, poor little girl. She had been seen by Mrs Conway going to her Grandfather's room and they had spoken. Mary, it seemed, had been pitifully grateful for all the kind enquiries and offers of assistance. She had confirmed that Dr Finter was satisfied that Monsieur Mercier was doing as well as could be expected. The poor thing, so young to undergo such stress, looked so unhappy and forlorn. Her eyes were red with weeping and it was obvious that she was under extraordinary strain. She had been so overcome her eyes had filled with tears when Mrs Conway had mentioned that eminent physician Sir Allan Setting would be her husband's guest for dinner, Mr Jepson having kindly offered to give up his place in the hope that Sir Allan might be willing to pay a purely informal call on her grandfather while the lodgers were enjoying a sherry. Mrs Conway made it plain that she and her husband thought it best to wait until after Sir Allan's visit to mention Mary to

Colin. Everybody understood perfectly, the poor boy was so emotionally upset.

The information about Mary was relayed in confidential whispers from one person to another shortly after six o'clock when Mrs Conway returned, resplendent in a silk dress and fur stole, to wait the arrival of Sir Allan while Mr Conway, worried about the boy, accompanied Colin to his room to wash and change for dinner. As the two men went down the passage, Fred Suddern, obviously waiting, stepped out with unusual determination and tried to waylay Colin. Mr Conway with equally unusual affability, magnanimously accepted Mr Suddern's invitation for a few words and allowed Colin to proceed to his room. His attitude as well as his words were fatherly.

'Go ahead, lad. I'll catch you up in a minute. We haven't much time.'

Colin went into his room and the man from Adelaide turned to Fred Suddern.

'Sorry, Suddern,' he said. 'Extraordinary this place today. One can't take a step without being held up for conversation, present company excepted of course. I must admit I haven't seen you before but the whole afternoon this place has swarmed like a hive of bees. Most extraordinary!'

'You're telling me!' Fred Suddern grunted.

'From your point of view it must be quite disturbing at a time like this. The old gentleman's condition has not deteriorated, I trust.'

Fred Suddern's face was flushed and his breath heavy.

'The same. I wanted a word with young Jepson,' he said.

'Oh, I wouldn't at the moment, Suddern,' Mr Conway advised. Although the door to Colin's room had closed, he lowered his voice.

'There's something the matter with the boy. He hasn't been eating, thought of avoiding dinner, handed his seat to my guest tonight – made me suspicious – a boy his age needs food.'

'He's a queer fish for an Aussie,' Fred said. 'What do you think his trouble is?'

'A girl, I'd say. He's got all the symptoms,' said the man from Adelaide. 'You know how it is at his age, and he's a long way from home. Well, glad nothing is worse on your front. See you later, Suddern.' He let himself in through Colin's door.

Conway sat in Colin's armchair for the time it took to smoke a pipe. Colin changed his suit, shirt and tie with impatience and all the time he grunted.

'Take it easy, son,' he was advised. 'Relax. You've made a good job of your part and Mum's made a beaut job of hers. Just have patience, boy, have patience.'

'I haven't seen Mary all day.'

'Rough, but the day's not finished. Take my word, lad, take my word! And hurry up. I don't want to miss meeting Sir Allan.'

'I'm ready. You go ahead, sir. I'll be on your heels.'

Conway went out the door and behind him Colin stopped to turn his key in the lock. But he did not catch up with the man from Adelaide. Victor Huston walked up to him before he reached the lounge. He had obviously been waiting and his manner was suave and steely.

'Ah, Mr Jepson, I must speak to you. Would you mind stepping into the office a moment?'

'Sorry, Mr Huston,' Colin replied. 'I'll see you later if you don't mind. Mr and Mrs Conway are waiting for me in the lounge. They have a guest. I can't hold up the party.'

Victor Huston planted himself with considerable force directly in front of Colin.

'Here will do just as well, Mr Jepson. I am sorry, I must ask for your room this evening. Your money will be refunded entirely, of course, and you will have been our guest for the time you have been here to make up for any inconvenience you may have suffered.'

'Inconvenience?' Colin, raising his voice repeated the word in a shrill shout. 'Inconvenience! You intend to throw me out at a moment's notice and you call it inconvenience. For what reason, may I ask?'

'Unfortunately, Mr Jepson, Miss Mercier did not consult her uncle or myself before she let the room. She did not know, of course, as we wished to spare her, that it would be necessary for a medical attendant to be near her grandfather from now on.'

Colin squared his shoulders and looked down from his superior height, straight into the eyes of Victor Huston.

'I understand, Mr Huston, that Miss Mercier's grandfather owns this establishment and that Mr Suddern is the manager. Therefore if circumstances are as you say, I shall expect to be told so by Mr Suddern or Miss Mercier herself.'

'Mr Jepson,' Victor Huston's voice was a low but menacing sneer. 'What kind of a man are you to refuse such a request at a time like this? The old man is at death's door. Arrangements have been made for Dr Finter to sleep here. The doctor and Mr Suddern are in the lounge. If you wish to be embarrassed...' He stepped aside. Colin darted forward and with Mr Huston behind him, arrived at the open lounge-room door.

The Conways' guest had arrived. Miss McKinnon was at the point of introducing Sir Allan Setting to Fred Suddern, having accomplished with pride, the introduction of this famous guest to Dr Finter.

Morris was approaching the door.

Victor Huston pushed Colin in as Morris went out. Immediately Dr August Finter excused himself and walked towards Huston. Fred Suddern remained where he was. His eyes were glazed and he looked a little drunk. Huston passed the doctor and confronted Suddern.

'Fred,' Huston said, 'there's a small matter, if you please...'

Colin took his opportunity and crossed the room to stand beside the man from Adelaide.

'Here is this young colleague of mine,' Conway greeted him. 'Sir Allan Setting – Colin Jepson.'

'How do you do, sir.'

'What happened to you?' Conway demanded, 'You were right behind me.'

'Huston stopped me and asked me to leave – tonight. It seems Dr Finter is about to move in and is to be given my room.'

'What's that you say?' Sir Allan grunted, while the ladies gasped.

'Move in – the doctor move in? Is he a relative? Mr Conway I believe gave me to understand the young lady was the only relative and the proprietor no more than her uncle by marriage, not her legal guardian.'

'That is true, sir,' Colin replied as Conway removed the pipe from his mouth.

'Otherwise, young man, my position would be quite unethical. I would not have agreed to see the patient. Is this doctor a relative?'

'No sir.'

'Then I fail to see why he is moving in,' remarked Conway mildly. 'Did Miss Mercier ask him such an unusual favour, Mr Suddern?'

Huston, steely-eyed, addressed himself to the man from Adelaide.

'That sounded rather an impertinence, Mr Conway. You appear to be interfering in a family matter between Mr Suddern and his niece.'

Conway shrugged. 'My apologies, Suddern, I will ask Miss Mercier when she comes in.' He kept his eyes on Huston.

'I think, Mr Conway, you have overstayed your welcome unless I am mistaken in assuming from Sir Allan's conversation, that you have had the presumption to invite him without my knowledge to visit my fiancée's grandfather.'

'Quite right, Mr Huston, quite right.' Conway beamed. 'Except for one thing. I have Miss Mercier's permission. The young lady is delighted to have such a distinguished physician attend her equally distinguished grandfather.'

'Without informing or consulting Dr Finter? I am surprised you should embarrass Sir Allan with such a request. It is to say the least, in Sir Allan's own words, unethical.'

'Not in the least, Huston, not in the least.' The man from Adelaide paused, the guests drew in their breath.

'You see it has not been possible to be ethical. Your friend Dr August Finter is not on the medical register.'

As he spoke, Morris arrived at the doorway. Behind her, in a green silk dress, stood Mary Mercier. Huston stepped two paces back and faced the door.

'You have gone too far, Conway,' he growled.

'Dr Finter is an old family friend from South Africa. Morris, please show Sir Allan Setting out. I do not wish to embarrass him further.

He has been the victim of particularly obnoxious circumstances. Good evening, Sir Allan. I hope you will accept my apologies.

Morris stepped up to Sir Allan Setting and Mary followed her into the room.

'This way, sir,' Morris said. 'Your overcoat is in the hall, sir.'

Without a glance at any member of the company, Sir Allan followed Morris. Politely, and with complete composure, Morris turned and closed the double doors behind her.

'Now,' Huston said icily, 'I hope the other guests will excuse me. Mr Conway and Mr Jepson, you will note that on your accounts and on your receipts there is a notice that informs you that the management reserves the right to terminate. Any money owing to you will be returned by Mr Suddern immediately after dinner.

'Uncle Fred!' Mary cried, 'Uncle Fred, what is going on? What has happened? Why is Victor sending everyone away?'

Fred Suddern did not answer. Miss McKinnon prompted him.

'Mr Suddern, your niece, let alone the rest of us, feel entitled to an explanation.'

Victor Huston moved towards Mary but Colin Jepson was at her side before him.

'My dear Mary,' Huston said. 'You are distraught. Please go back to your room. I will explain everything later when your grandfather is better and you are less upset.'

'But I have just come from Grandfather, Victor. He is exactly the same as he usually is, no better and no worse.'

Huston's voice altered. 'Will you take her please, Dr Finter?'

'What do you mean?'

'Certainly, Mr Huston,' Finter replied suavely. 'I must go to your grandfather, Miss Mercier, and I may need your help.'

'Please, Mary,' Fred Suddern spoke for the first time, lurching forward a little. 'It's better if you go with the doctor. You know that if you don't go, I'll have to.'

Standing with Colin beside her, Mary looked from one face to another around the room. A tremor seemed to run through her body. Quite suddenly she moved to the door as lithely as a panther. But she turned with her back against it and threw her arms wide.

'Don't let them go to my grandfather,' she cried out. 'Don't let them near him. I don't trust them. Don't let them go.'

Huston stepped towards her. His voice hissed as soft as a snake but as deadly.

'Get away from that door, Mary.'

'Get away yourself,' Colin Jepson snapped and hit him solidly with all the pent-up energy of an inactive day so that he fell backwards to the floor. Conway, with the delight of a small boy, grappled with the doctor and all the women shrieked. A momentary bedlam ensued, in the midst of which the door was pushed open behind Mary, and Morris with Sir Allan Setting stood framed in it.

'I see, my dear Conway,' the deep voice of the physician boomed above the din, 'that you have made an active move in the right direction. I commend your effort and suggest that the combined company detain the so-called management of this establishment until the police arrive.'

'Detainment arranged, sir,' Colin called, 'at least temporarily. Morris, have you got any rope? It looks like Huston's coming around.'

'Indeed, Mr Jepson!' Miss McKinnon remarked tartly. 'Perhaps you could give an explanation as to what right you have to tie up Mr Huston or, for that matter, why you had to hit him in the first place, even admitting his pugnacious attitude?'

'Madam,' commanded the sonorous voice of Sir Allan Setting. 'If you please, do not distract Mr Jepson. Explanations will follow in due course. Conway, I congratulate you on your detection. The patient I just visited has been persistently and relentlessly drugged. A wicked case, as wicked as I have seen since the war.'

'Good-o,' said the man from Adelaide, who held a protesting Dr Finter in a state of immobility.

'And what is good about it?' demanded Miss McKinnon.

'Will somebody get a rope?' Colin repeated. 'I have just relieved Huston of a revolver. Will you take it to Mr Conway, Mary.'

'A revolver!' Miss McKinnon shrieked, 'then knock him out again, Mr Jepson.'

It was Morris who noticed that Fred Suddern had edged his way almost to the door. With commendable speed for a woman of her size, she confronted him with blazing eyes.

'Would you be going somewhere, sir?' she hissed at him. 'For another drink perhaps – selling yourself body and soul for beer and the horses, proposin' to make a respectable woman like me mistress of the manager's quarters, when I'm for runnin' the place as it is. I warned you that you'd end up losing the rooms and your job. A good place you had here, paid for by that poor old man. Better than you deserve, cheatin' your own sister's child with those bloodsuckers.'

Fred Suddern backed before her fury, his flushed face bemused with desire for the drink she denied him. Someone pushed a chair behind his knees and, collapsing into it, he stared in stupefied resentment at the snow-white apron bib Morris wore under her second chin.

The voice of Mary Mercier commanded with compassion and pity.

'You mustn't be upset, Morris. Uncle Fred has had too much to drink. He has to drink because he's weak, that is all. I doubt he was running away.'

'Whereas Mr Huston here,' said the man from Adelaide, pointing with his foot, 'is an international criminal I have been after for some time. There is an Australian embezzlement charge he will have to face, dating back a few years before he switched his activities to possible diamond leases in the Congo.'

'Diamonds!' the company gasped in fascinated unison.

'Being the price they are, and in consideration of their constant popularity among a certain section of the community,' Mr Conway explained with a sly look at Colin, 'diamonds make it well worthwhile to acquire the estate of an old gentleman from Kasai province, the so-called diamond state of the poor besieged Congo, by the unsavoury and unsuspected method of marrying his grand-daughter. Miss Mercier, if Morris should open the front door, Mr Jepson and I could be relieved of a pair of scoundrels by a couple of burly types from Scotland Yard who happen to be waiting outside. Once they have taken over, I feel the guests present might relax over dinner before the usual questioning procedures. You are still, I presume, Sir Allan, happy to be guest of my wife and me at dinner? Mr Jepson doubtless will dine with Miss Mercier.'

As the policemen came in, Colin stood up, and looked at Mary Mercier. She may have been pale but her skin denied it. Perhaps she was terrified but the shining eyes that returned his gaze were so honey-sweet he could not wonder that she had fooled her grandfather about lions during all her childhood years.

'There will be time to see your grandfather now if you wish, my dear,' Sir Allan was saying. 'Then we will get him off to the hospital before the questioning.'

'Come along, Colin,' Mary said, her voice camouflaging her feelings, both proud and impervious.

Colin, among all those present, even including the man from Adelaide, was the only one who knew what to do besides obey. He smiled and took her hand.

'Come along yourself, honey-eyes,' he said, and the tension rushed out of Mary Mercier to make room for the blush which flowed into her cheeks.

oooOOOooo

Kathryn Purnell was born in Vancouver, Canada in 1911. She travelled by sea to Australia with her family as a young woman. During the voyage she met and later married Australian scientist William (Bill) Purnell.

Kathryn embodied the soul and spirit of a creative writer. She maintained an intense interest in everything around her, the natural and spiritual worlds, the everyday and the eternal, diverse countries and their cultures, as well as the human condition (of which she had an uncanny understanding). A gifted educator, she was an inspiration to many aspiring writers to whom she taught creative writing. She believed intensely in the need to encourage women writers, the constraints on whom she felt herself at a very personal level.

Bill Purnell's work in the early years of UNESCO as head of its Science Cooperation Division took Kathryn to Paris to live in the immediate post war years, then to Cairo and later Jakarta. She travelled widely in Europe and later spent time in South Africa. Her husband's ill health compelled the family to return permanently to Australia in the late nineteen fifties, It was particularly in this period of her life, with the common pressures of maintaining a family, supporting a husband in his professional life and finding time to create, that she felt most strongly the constraints and limitations placed on the female creative spirit by the societal practices and beliefs of the time.

But create she did, both poetry and prose work. She also spent much of her time teaching aspiring writers, mostly women. Active in the Society of Women Writers, in 1998 she won The Alice Award, a biennial award for long-term and distinguished contribution to literature by an

Australian woman. Other awards included the State of Victoria Short Story Award and the Moomba Short Story Prize both in 1966/67 and The Society of Women Writers Poetry Prize in 1972. In addition to poetry, Kathryn left a fine legacy of prose writings, much of it unpublished. A current project seeks to redress this by publishing some of her novellas, short stories and her singular novel.

ALSO BY KATHRYN PURNELL

PROSE
The Augustinian Correspondence
In an Urban Forest
Apollo in January
Sam in July

POETRY
Safari
Pandora
Harpsichord of Water
Otway Country
Fairy Trees: Poems for the Fitzroy Gardens